Margaret
and The Pope
Go to Assisi

THE POPE'S CAT SERIES

*The story of a stray that was born
on the Via della Conciliazione in Rome,
was adopted by the Pope, and how she then runs the
Vatican from museum to floorboard. For ages six and up.*

This volume is preceded by

The Pope's Cat

Margaret's Night in St. Peter's (A Christmas Story)

Margaret's First Holy Week

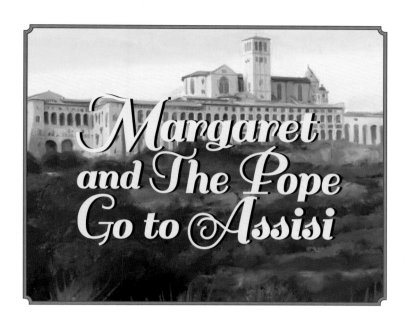

Margaret and The Pope Go to Assisi

JON M. SWEENEY
Illustrated by ROY DeLEON

PARACLETE PRESS
BREWSTER, MASSACHUSETTS

2020 First Printing

Margaret and the Pope Go to Assisi

Text copyright © 2020 by Jon M. Sweeney

Illustrations copyright © 2020 by Roy DeLeon

ISBN 978-1-64060-170-3

The Paraclete Press name and logo (dove on cross) are trademarks of Paraclete Press, Inc.

Library of Congress Cataloging-in-Publication Data.
Names: Sweeney, Jon M., 1967- author. | DeLeon, Roy, illustrator.
Title: Margaret and the Pope go to Assisi / Jon M. Sweeney ; illustrated by Roy DeLeon.
Description: Brewster, Massachusetts : Paraclete Press, [2020] | Series:
    The Pope's cat ; 4 | Summary: "Margaret the cat and the Pope travel
    together by train to Assisi. They visit the town where St. Francis of
    Assisi lived his life, now a place of pilgrimage for many people"--
    Provided by publisher.
Identifiers: LCCN 2019038107 (print) | LCCN 2019038108 (ebook) | ISBN
    9781640601703 (trade paperback) | ISBN 9781640604407 (mobi) | ISBN
    9781640604414 (epub) | ISBN 9781640604421 (pdf)
Subjects: LCSH: Francis, of Assisi, Saint, 1182-1226--Juvenile fiction. |
    CYAC: Francis, of Assisi, Saint, 1182-1226--Fiction. | Cats--Fiction. |
    Popes--Fiction. | Catholics--Fiction. | Christian life--Fiction.
Classification: LCC PZ7.1.S9269 Maj 2020 (print) | LCC PZ7.1.S9269
    (ebook) | DDC [E]--dc23
LC record available at https://lccn.loc.gov/2019038107
LC ebook record available at https://lccn.loc.gov/2019038108

10 9 8 7 6 5 4 3 2 1

Published by Paraclete Press
Brewster, Massachusetts
www.paracletepress.com
Printed in Canada

For Franciscans everywhere
—Jon

---

*For Brother Sun and Sister Moon, Brothers
Wind and Air, Sister Water, Brother Fire, and
for Mother Earth*
—Roy

CHAPTER 1

W here is she?" said the Vatican's director of television broadcasting, as he walked into the Pope's outer office. "Where did she go?" He sounded a little bit angry.

"Where did *who* go, Mr. Director?" Father Felipe said. Felipe noticed the director was still wearing his headphones, and there were cords dragging all over the floor behind him.

"His Holiness's cat!" the director replied.

"Has something happened involving Margaret?" Felipe said. But he already imagined what was taking place. Margaret had gotten herself into trouble—again.

"We were broadcasting the Pope's Wednesday general audience when that cat started rubbing her head against one of the microphones."

"Then, she ran up to His Holiness, interrupting his homily."

"Oh, it was just awful!" the director said, clenching his fists.

He was so worked up, recounting what *that cat* had done, that his face had turned red. He looked as if he might pop like a balloon.

Felipe smiled.

Felipe knew what the Pope would say, and he knew exactly where Margaret would be hiding.

The Pope's apartment has very large closets, because Popes have many clothes, and most of the clothes need to be hung on hangers.

There are, for example, the white cassocks—long coats that begin almost at his ears and go down to his ankles. He wears a white cassock almost every day.

There is also the white stole, embroidered with crosses, often draped over his shoulders.

There is the little cap (*"zucchetto"* it is called, in Italian). A Pope's *zucchetto* is white. Cardinals wear red ones, and if a priest or a deacon wears one, it is always black.

And don't forget the mitre—a ceremonial hat that the Pope wears only on very special occasions!

Since the Pope met Margaret on the streets of Rome, adopted her, and brought her inside the Vatican, Margaret has made a comfortable home for herself in his apartment. She has made the couches her best napping spots. There's the table by the window she loves to sit on, where she can easily see down into St. Peter's Square. And . . . she has adopted one of the Pope's large closets as her secret hiding place.

It was there she was hiding, in that closet, when Father Felipe went looking for her.

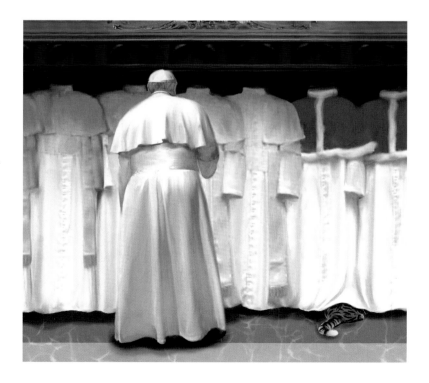

Arrivederci, in Italian, means "See you later." Father Felipe said "*Arrivederci*" to the television director.

Then he closed the outer door to the Pope's apartment.

Walking to the other end of the large room, he opened one of the tall closet doors.

Gently moving a couple of cassocks out of the way with his hand, Felipe could then see all the way to the back of the closet.

There sat Margaret. She looked up at Felipe.

Father Felipe bent down and picked Margaret up. The smile on his face said that everything was okay.

Just then, the Pope walked into the room.

"Is Margaret okay?" the Pope said. He walked toward the closet. He looked in, peering closely at his beloved.

"Don't worry, *Amore mio.*" (*Amore mio* means "My love.") "People can be so fussy, can't they?" he said, picking her up in his arms.

CHAPTER 2

I have some wonderful news!" the Pope said, looking at Margaret and Father Felipe. "We are going to the city of Saint Francis!"

"Wonderful, Holy Father. But what is the occasion?" Felipe asked.

"A World Day of Prayer for Peace," the Pope said. "We are gathering religious leaders from all over the world to join us in praying for peace on every continent, in every country, and among all people."

The Pope seemed very excited, and that made Margaret excited, too.

"I will begin to make the arrangements," said Father Felipe, dutifully.

"I've already taken care of things," said the Pope.

"Well . . . when do we go?" Felipe asked.

"In one week," the Pope said.

Now, some of the Roman Curia—the people whose job it is to assist the Pope in administrating all the congregations, councils, and offices of the universal Roman Catholic Church—were not happy with the details and plans for the trip to Assisi. The Pope, for instance, decided on his own that he wouldn't be driven in a car.

He wanted to take the train.

"But the train is not safe, Your Holiness," some in the Curia said.

"It is not suitable for the Holy See." ("Holy See" is another way of saying, "Authority of a Pope.")

Others said, "The train will take so much longer, Holy Father."

"That's okay," the Pope replied, "I'm not in a hurry. Also, you shouldn't worry so much."

A week later, the Pope was holding Margaret in his arms as they stepped out of a small car arriving at the train station. People were rushing here and there, loading things onto the train, saying goodbye to loved ones and friends, locating the proper car according to their tickets.

Father Felipe was there, carrying an armful of papers. A few Curia officials were there, too. Even the Vatican's director of television broadcasting seemed to be arriving at the train for the trip to Assisi. (Margaret didn't see him as they were boarding.)

Inside the train, the Pope, Margaret, Felipe, and a few others traveling with the Pope were shown to a private car.

There, on one of the seats, was a large cat carrier with a fluffy pillow inside. The Pope nuzzled Margaret, and she nuzzled him back. Then he opened the little door on the carrier and placed Margaret inside. "You'll be safe and comfortable in here," he said, closing the door.

The Pope was right. Margaret settled right down into that pillow.

A few minutes later, the train started to move, and a few minutes after that, the chooga chooga chooga sound, and the gentle rattling feeling of the train on the tracks, helped Margaret quickly fall fast asleep.

CHAPTER 3

Margaret was just waking up when the train pulled into the station of Assisi.

"The home of Saint Francis!" the Pope said. "Wake up, Margaret. I want to show you this magical city."

He opened the door of the cat carrier and Margaret promptly jumped on top of it, so that she could better see out the train windows.

She saw in the distance the beautiful, hilltop city where the world's most famous saint was born and died 800 years ago.

The sun was setting, just then, and Mount Subasio, which towers above Assisi, was shining in hues of pink and orange.

"Brother Sun is glowing with joy," the Pope said.

Margaret was confused. *Brother who?*

The Pope clarified: "Saint Francis wrote poems and songs praising God in all of God's Creation, including *Brother* Sun, *Sister* Moon, *Brother* Wind, and *Sister* Water."

Margaret was still a little bit confused.

"Come on," the Pope said, picking her up. Felipe and the others were close by.

"Our first stop is the Basilica di San Francesco." (Now, "*di San Francesco*" simply means "of Saint Francis" in Italian.)

They climbed into a car that would take them up the hill to the great church where the scenes of Saint Francis's life are painted on the walls, and where his body is buried beneath the high altar.

When they arrived at the Basilica, they were greeted by men in brown cassocks, tied at their waists with cords. They were Franciscans, men who live in the friary that is attached to the Basilica of Saint Francis of Assisi.

The Pope greeted each man with a hug, and each of the Franciscans kissed the Pope's hand.

Then the Pope went to a microphone. He began to deliver a short talk to the friars, speaking from notes he'd written while riding in the train from Rome.

Margaret heard the Pope say how good it was for the men to be "little before God," and to be "gentle wherever they go," just as their founder, Saint Francis, was little and gentle. She liked that.

Margaret tried to keep listening to the Pope's speech, but after a few minutes she found it difficult to concentrate.

Then she spied a long hallway leading out of the friary, and she became curious. No one seemed to notice when Margaret left where they all were standing.

She continued down the hallway until she reached a dimly lit stairwell. There, she saw a long line of people slowly making their way down into a dark room below. No one was talking while descending. As Margaret would discover later, these were pilgrims on their way to the crypt. She might have been scared, if she had known this, then. Crypts are where people are buried. But she wouldn't have been scared by the relative darkness. Cats, as you probably realize, can see better than humans can, in the dark.

Cats are also small and agile. Margaret easily scooted and scampered her way through the quiet crowd, down those stairs, and into the small hall. There was very little light down there, even though many candles were lit.

The long line of people continued moving toward the front of the room, in a gentle circle around the place marked as where Saint Francis is buried.

Some of the people were lighting candles. Others were praying. One young man was praying with a rosary. There was a man in a black jacket whispering *"Silenzio"* ("Silence") to anyone who was talking.

Margaret stepped up to a young girl who was kneeling beside her mother. Margaret put her paws on the stone ledge beside the girl. They looked at each other, and the girl rubbed Margaret under her chin.

Then the girl, her mother, and Margaret got up and moved on. It seemed that others needed a turn to kneel in that spot.

As she made the circle all the way around the place where Saint Francis is buried, Margaret saw the names of four of Francis's best friends, who also lived 800 years ago, and are buried there beside him: Brother Leo, Brother Masseo, Brother Rufino, and Brother Angelo.

CHAPTER 4

W hile Margaret was away, the Pope had finished his speech, and he walked outside, around to the front of the Upper Church of the Basilica, to greet the distinguished guests who were beginning to arrive.

Margaret saw the Pope when she came back up the stairs from the crypt, then up another long flight of stairs from the Lower Church, into the sunlight. She ran over to him, and he picked her up.

"Did you have an interesting adventure?" he whispered in her ear. She purrrred.

The religious leaders were arriving.

The Anglican Archbishop of Canterbury was there, wearing a cassock, similar to the one the Pope was wearing, but in purple.

Then there was H. H. the Dalai Lama, leader of the Tibetan people, who had just come from India. He was dressed in saffron.

The Grand Imam had just arrived from Egypt. He also wore a type of white cap on his head.

Distinguished rabbis were arriving from the United States, Europe, South America, and Israel. Both men and women, they were all wearing black or blue suits, and they had black caps on their heads.

Russian Orthodox, Greek Orthodox, Armenian Orthodox, and other bishops of the Orthodox churches were also standing in front of the Upper Church of the Basilica of St. Francis. The Pope greeted each person with a brotherly embrace.

"Your Holiness," Father Felipe said to the Pope, so that everyone could hear, "We are ready for you inside. It is time to begin."

"Thank you, Father," the Pope said, and he smiled at everyone who had come, and said to them all in a loud voice, "Brothers and sisters, please join me inside the church."

Inside the Upper Church, Margaret saw rows and rows of chairs, pitchers of water, tables and flowers, and members of the press holding microphones and notepads.

The Vatican director of television was standing near the front of the room. He had headphones on his ears, and he seemed to be talking into a microphone attached to the headset.

Then Margaret noticed something else—something much more startling. The walls! Everywhere she looked—and she was turning around and around to see them—were the most amazing paintings covering the walls of the Upper Church of the Basilica.

As you may know, cats don't usually pay attention to paintings. But these seemed special.

Cats do notice other things, however, and as the Pope was about to speak from the microphone, and as she heard the director of television say to Father Felipe, "We're ready," Margaret saw a mouse poke its head out of a tiny crack in the wall. Her attention quickly turned to the twitching of that little mouse.

The Pope began: "Here in this room, brothers and sisters, where the great artist Giotto long ago captured the scenes of the life of Saint Francis, the little poor man of peace, we gather to affirm our commitment to peace in our own day, and to take this commitment back to our religious communities, our people, our countries, and our leaders."

Margaret hopped onto an available chair at the end of the first row. She wanted to listen.

And she did listen. She forgot about the mouse. But, the chair was comfortable, so comfortable, and the room was warm, and cats—well, you know,

cats like

to

sleep.

So before the Pope was even halfway

through his talk,

Margaret began

to quietly

s n o r e .

CHAPTER 5

The following day, the Pope announced to Margaret and Father Felipe: "We should go for a walk in town. We have an hour or so before everyone gathers again to talk and pray."

Felipe noticed that the Pope was wearing a jacket over his white cassock.

"Very good, Your Holiness," he said. "I will alert the police so that they may begin to make the area safe."

"That's not necessary," the Pope said. "I want to see the people of Assisi as they are." And he picked up Margaret and left the room. Felipe ran after him.

Within a few minutes, the Basilica of Saint Francis behind them, the Pope and Margaret and Father Felipe were walking on the medieval stone streets of Assisi.

"Saint Francis did so many interesting things," the Pope was saying. "Let's look for evidence of him."

No one noticed the three of them, at least for a little while.

Soon, they came upon a group of girls and boys playing in a piazza near the center of town. Some were laughing. Others were eating gelato. Gelato is a special kind of Italian ice cream, made from milk and sugar.

Margaret saw the children with the gelato, and she began to lick her lips. She hadn't tasted gelato in a long, long time. The Pope heard Margaret beginning to purr.

"Would you like some gelato, my dear?" he asked. She looked up at him and meowed. If you were there, just then, you would have thought for sure that they were talking with each other!

Margaret wanted hazelnut.

As she licked her gelato from a cup (no cone), Margaret noticed that one of the children was being quiet. There were children all around this boy, and he smiled sometimes, but then he seemed to be looking for something, or simply thinking quietly to himself.

The Pope noticed the boy, too. He said to Margaret, "Maybe he is a little lonely." Now how did the Pope know Margaret was thinking about that boy?

"That boy is like Saint Francis," the Pope went on.

"Francis was the center of attention, always having fun, until he began to look inside himself, and all around himself, for something more special than the ordinary. He would find that something special in his relationship with God."

Their gelato gone, they kept walking. Children were now following them, because people started to realize that the Pope was walking down their street. That doesn't happen every day—even in Italy!

Soon they came to a row of street vendors, and one of them was selling birds. Gray pigeons and white doves cooed in cages upon a small table.

"Saint Francis preached to birds!" the Pope said with excitement, at the sight of the beautiful creatures.

"There were times when people did not want to listen to what it means to follow Christ, so he turned to the birds and said to them: 'Sing! Sing for your Creator!'"

Margaret paid very close attention to the birds. Cats, you see, are the natural enemies of birds. Cats eat birds. Margaret's mouth began to water. The gelato had been delicious, but now she began to imagine tasting one of those pigeons or doves!

The Pope picked Margaret up in his arms, and walked over to the cages. "You know what else Saint Francis did, Margaret?"

She was anxiously waiting for the answer.

"He bought birds from a vendor on a street just like this—" the Pope said, handing the man some money. Then, opening the cage, the Pope continued— "Simply in order to release them, and let them go free!"

The Pope took a step backward, and motioned with his hand for the doves to leave the cage. Margaret watched them as, one by one, they stepped to the edge of the cage, toward the open door. The Pope gently picked them up in his large hands, raised his hands above his head, and said, "Go, sisters and brothers! Be free to love and serve your Creator!"

Margaret watched as the birds flew up into the sky toward Brother Sun and Mount Subasio.

EPILOGUE

They went on that day to see many other things in Assisi that reminded the Pope of Saint Francis.

They saw where Francis was born, and the house in which he grew up.

They saw where Francis was baptized.

They prayed in the Basilica of Saint Clare—where Clare, a good friend of Francis's, and the first woman to become a Franciscan, is buried. There in the chapel is the San Damiano cross from which Francis first heard God speak to him. Francis heard God say, "Go and rebuild my church." That's what Saint Francis did.

"We would visit the Carceri—the caves on Mount Subasio where Francis used to go alone to pray—if we had the time," the Pope said to Margaret and Father Felipe.

But Margaret was glad they didn't have time to go there. She thought she might be afraid of what lives in caves!

Before long, they were back at the Basilica of Saint Francis. All the religious leaders from around the world were gathered there again, and the prayer event was about to continue.

The Pope walked into the room. He started his remarks that day by saying, "Friends, as Saint Francis used to say to ordinary people on the street: Peace and all good. That is what I wish for all of us, and that is what I hope we all will be in the world."

THE END

ABOUT THE AUTHOR

Jon M. Sweeney is an author, husband, and father of four. He has been interviewed on many television programs including CBS Saturday Morning, Fox News, and PBS's Religion and Ethics Newsweekly. His popular history *The Pope Who Quit: A True Medieval Tale of Mystery, Death, and Salvation* was optioned by HBO. He's the author of thirty-five other books, including *The Complete Francis of Assisi, When Saint Francis Saved the Church*, the winner of an award in history from the Catholic Press Association, and *The Enthusiast: How the Best Friend of Francis of Assisi Almost Destroyed What He Started*. This is his fourth book for children. He presents often at literary and religious conferences, and churches, writes regularly for *America* in the US and *The Tablet* in the UK, and is active on social media (Twitter @jonmsweeney; Facebook jonmsweeney).

ABOUT THE ILLUSTRATOR

Roy DeLeon is an Oblate of St. Benedict, a spiritual director, a workshop facilitator focused on creative praying, an Urban Sketcher, and a professional illustrator. In addition to illustrating *The Pope's Cat* series, he is also the author of *Praying with the Body: Bringing the Psalms to Life*. He lives in Bothell, Washington, with his wife, Annie.

The Pope's **CAT** series

ISBN 978-1-61261-935-4
$9.99

In case you're wondering how the Pope and Margaret first met . . .

This is the book where it all started—the story of Margaret when she was a stray cat on the Via della Conciliazione in Rome, how she was adopted by the Pope, and then began running the Vatican from museum to floorboard.

COMING IN 2021

The fifth episode in this story, a prequel....

BEFORE *Margaret* MET THE POPE
Story of a Conclave

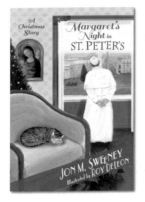

ISBN 978-1-61261-936-1
$10.99

In this delightful new story from their lives, the Pope takes Margaret on a tour of St. Peter's. But when he's called away to work, Margaret becomes lost in the world's largest church. She meets saints, children, tourists, and the artist Michelangelo's famous statue, the Pietà, before being reunited with the Pope as Midnight Mass is about to begin.

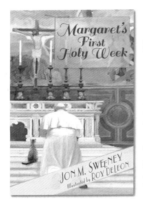

ISBN 978-1-61261-937-8
$9.99

This adventure has Margaret watching the Pope, experiencing Holy Week in the Vatican and Rome. From the joy of Palm Sunday in St. Peter's Square, to foot-washing in a Roman prison, the solemnity of Good Friday, and the expectation of Easter, this playful story explores serious things.